King & Kayla

and the Case of the
Mysterious Mouse

Written by
Dori Hillestad Butler

Illustrated by
Nancy Meyers

PEACHTREE
ATLANTA

For my friend, Kellye.

And page 39 is for Cosmo.

—D. H. B.

To Connie and Scout, who love to jump fences

—N. M.

Published by
PEACHTREE PUBLISHERS
1700 Chattahoochee Avenue
Atlanta, Georgia 30318-2112
www.peachtree-online.com

Text © 2017 Dori Hillestad Butler
Illustrations © 2017 Nancy Meyers
First trade paperback edition published in 2018

Edited by Kathy Landwehr
Design and composition by Nicola Simmonds Carmack
The illustrations were drawn in pencil, with color added digitally.

Printed in March 2018 by RR Donnelley, China
10 9 8 7 6 5 4 3 2 (hardcover)
10 9 8 7 6 5 4 3 2 1 (trade paperback)
HC: 978-1-56145-879-0
PB: 978-1-68263-017-4

Library of Congress Cataloging-in-Publication Data

Names: Butler, Dori Hillestad, author. | Meyers, Nancy, 1961- illustrator.
Title: King and Kayla and the case of the mysterious mouse / written by
    Dori Hillestad Butler ; illustrated by Nancy Meyers.
Description: First edition. | Atlanta, Georgia : Peachtree Publishers, [2017]
    | Summary: When King's favorite blue ball goes missing, he and Kayla
    must put together clues to figure out where it went.
Identifiers: LCCN 2016047534 | ISBN 9781561458790
Subjects: | CYAC: Dogs—Fiction. | Balls (Sporting goods)—Fiction. |
    Lost and found possessions—Fiction. | Mystery and detective stories.
Classification: LCC PZ7.B9759 Kio 2017 | DDC [E]—dc23
LC record available at *https://lccn.loc.gov/2016047534*

Contents

Chapter One

Fetch!

Hello!

My name is King. I'm a dog.

This is Kayla. She is my human.

Kayla and I are at Jillian's house.
We're playing fetch with Jillian
and Thor.

I LOVE fetch. It's

my favorite thing!

Kayla throws the ball. I run...run...
RUN after it.

"Got it!" I tell Kayla with my tail. I
LOVE my ball. It's my favorite thing!

I bring it back to Kayla. "Throw it again," I say.

"You're so lucky your dog can fetch," Jillian says.

"Thor will learn to fetch when he gets bigger," Kayla says.

"I'm already big," Thor says. "And I can fetch. Watch!" Thor picks up my ball and runs away with it.

That is NOT how you play fetch.

"Bring it, Thor!" Jillian claps her hands together. "Bring me the ball!"

"Oh, look! A butterfly!" Thor says.
He drops the ball and chases the
butterfly.

My ball rolls under a bush. Jillian
crawls under to get it. Then she throws
it to Kayla.

But she throws too hard. My ball sails
over the fence.

"Sorry," Jillian says. "I'll go get it." She
runs next door.

I wait by the gate. I wait…and wait…
and WAIT.

Finally, Jillian comes back with a ball.
But it's not *my* ball.

Chapter Two

It's Not My Ball

"Here you go, King!" Jillian says. She tosses the ball to me.

This ball smells like another dog. It smells like another dog's food. This is not my ball.

"Bring it, King," Kayla says. "Bring me the ball."

"It's not my ball," I say. I don't want to bring Kayla a ball that isn't mine.

"I'll get it!
I'll get it!"
Thor says.

He pounces on
the ball.

"Oh, look! A bird!" Thor says. He
drops the ball and chases the bird.

"What's wrong, King?" Kayla asks. "Why won't you bring me the ball?"

"It's not my ball," I say again.

"Wait a minute," Kayla says. She picks up the ball. "This isn't King's ball."

"Sure it is. It's small and blue," Jillian says.

"But there are no teeth marks," Kayla says. "King's ball is old. This one is brand new."

I wag my tail. Kayla is a good detective.

"Come on, King," Kayla says. "Let's go find your ball."

We go next door.

I count one…seven…four balls in this yard. But none of them are mine. Where's my ball?

I look under the bushes.
No ball.

I look around the garden.
No ball.

Sniff...sniff...
I smell something!
Something BAD.
It's under the porch.

I look under the porch.
Two eyes stare back at me.

Chapter Three

Cat with No Name

It's a cat! There's a cat under this porch.

"Go away, Dog," the cat says.

"My name isn't Dog. It's King," I tell the cat. "What's your name?"

The cat doesn't answer. Maybe he doesn't have a name.

"I'm looking for my ball," I say. "Have you seen it?"

The cat just licks his paw.

I've met this cat before. He came inside our
house once and stole some peanut butter treats.

I LOVE peanut butter
treats. They're my
favorite food!

Maybe he stole my ball.

"Did you steal my ball?"
I ask that cat with no name.

"No!" he says. "Mouse did. Now go away!"

Mouse? "What mouse?" I ask. "My ball
is bigger than a mouse. How could a
mouse have stolen my ball?"

Cat with No Name doesn't answer. He darts out from under the porch and races across the yard.

I chase him. "Tell me about the mouse!" I call.

"King!" Kayla yells at me. "Stop chasing that cat!"

My tail droops. I don't like it when Kayla yells at me.

"Let's go home and see if we can solve this mystery," Kayla says.

I follow Kayla back to our house.

We go inside and Kayla grabs a notebook and pencil. "Let's make a list of everything we *know* about this case," she says.

1. King's ball went over the fence.
2. Jillian brought back a ball, but it wasn't King's ball.
3. None of the other balls next door are King's.

If I could write, I would add this to Kayla's list of things we know:

There was a cat under the porch next door.

The cat said a mouse took my ball.

"Now let's make a list of what we *don't* know about this case," Kayla says.

1. Did King's ball roll away?
2. Did it land in a different yard?
3. Did someone come and take King's ball?

If I could write, I would add this to
Kayla's list of things we don't know:

How could a
mouse have
taken my ball?

"Now we need a plan,"
Kayla says.

I have a plan:

Find the
mouse!

Chapter Four

You're in Trouble!

The mouse must be next door.

But the gate is closed. How am I going to get over there? How am I going to find the mouse?

Hey, maybe I can jump the fence.

I run...run...RUN—

All of a sudden, Thor darts in front of me. "What are you doing?" he asks.

I skid to a stop. "Trying not to run you over," I say.

"Where are you going?" Thor asks.

"Can I come? I want to come! Please let me come!"

"Sorry," I tell Thor. "You're too little."

"I want to come! I want to come!" Thor yells. He jumps up and down.

Kayla and Jillian look over.

"I'll be back in a minute," I tell Kayla.

I run…run…RUN past Thor and leap over the fence.

"King! What are you doing? Bad dog!" Kayla screams.

I can't see her now. But I can hear her. I don't like it when Kayla says I'm a bad dog.

"I'm trying to solve this case," I tell Kayla.

Kayla opens the gate. "King! Come!"
she yells. She makes mad eyes at me.

I don't like it when Kayla makes mad
eyes at me.

But I have to find my ball.

Sniff...sniff...

Now where's that mouse?

Chapter Five

The Biggest, LOUDEST Dog in the World

Aha! A mouse hole!
I dig…dig…DIG!

None of these mice have my ball.
Where could it be?

Cat with No Name said a mouse
took it.

But guess what? Cats don't always
tell the truth.

Grrr! Where is that cat?

"King! Come!" Kayla yells. She chases me across the yard.

Cat with No Name isn't in the tree anymore.

Maybe he went back under the porch. Nope. He's not under there, either.

Hey, I smell my ball! Where is it? Sniff...sniff... I think it's up those stairs. And through that doggy door.

"No, King!" Kayla yells. "You can't go in someone else's house."

I can't stop myself. I charge through the doggy door.

I smell strange humans, a strange dog, and grilled cheese. I LOVE grilled cheese! It's my favorite food.

Then I see the strange dog.

"WHO ARE YOU?" he asks. "WHY ARE YOU IN MY HOUSE?"

He is the biggest, LOUDEST dog in the world.

"I'm King," I say. "I'm looking for my ball." I wag my tail to show I'm friendly.

"I'M MOUSE," he says. "I FOUND
YOUR BALL IN MY YARD."

Wait a minute! *He's* Mouse?
Cat with No Name was telling the truth.
Mouse took my ball. But Mouse isn't a
mouse. He's a dog. A dog *named* Mouse.

"HERE'S YOUR BALL," Mouse says.

Oh, boy! I'm so happy, happy, HAPPY
to see my ball!

"Let's play!"
I say.

We leap and play until Mouse's human walks into the room.

"Where did you come from? How did you get in here?" he asks.

"Through the doggy door," I say.

Ding-dong!

"SOMEONE'S HERE! SOMEONE'S HERE!" Mouse says.

We all run to the door.

It's Kayla and Jillian.

"I'm really sorry, but my dog accidentally ran into your house," Kayla tells Mouse's human. "He was looking for his ball."

Mouse's human smiles. "Looks like he found it. And it looks like our new dog has a new friend."

I wag my tail. I LOVE new friends. They're my favorite thing!

The End

Oh, boy! I LOVE books. They're my favorite things!

More great mysteries from King & Kayla

King & Kayla and the Case of the Missing Dog Treats

HC: $14.95 / 978-1-56145-877-6
PB: $6.95 / 978-1-68263-015-0

When some fresh-baked dog treats disappear, King sniffs out the clues to help Kayla find out what happened to them.

"…a great introduction to mysteries, gathering facts, and analytical thinking for an unusually young set."

—*Booklist*

King & Kayla and the Case of the Secret Code

HC: $14.95 / 978-1-56145-878-3
PB: $6.95 / 978-1-68263-016-7

Kayla receives a letter written in code.
What does it say?

"Each book allows plenty of room for predictions and provides a glimpse into the great payoff reading can deliver."

—*Horn Book Magazine*

King & Kayla and the Case of the Lost Tooth

HC: $14.95 / 978-1-56145-880-6
PB: $6.95 / 978-1-68263-018-1

Kayla lost a tooth—but now it's missing. Where did it go?

"This funny, endearing addition to the series will delight early readers, especially dog lovers." —*Kirkus Reviews*